HOW TO
SAVE A
RURAL MALL

(in three easy steps)

This edition published December 2024
Copyright 2022 © Marie Winters & Jo Richardson All Rights Reserved
Edited by Sue Bartelt
Cover Image and internal images from Dreamstime

ISBN: 9798332768286

TABLE OF CONTENTS

PART ONE

Black Friday

Today is the day.

Black Friday.

The official start of the Christmas season.

Candace Kane is set.

She's running on one hour of sleep and two pots of coffee but she's ready to launch her three-point plan to save the Oak Grove Mall. She's never been more certain of anything in her life.

She knows exactly how she's going to make it happen.

1) Overhaul Christmas Village,

2) Get the business owners on board,

3) And then, the piece de resistance, hire the best Santa the Oak Grove Mall has ever seen.

Candace steps out of the office and takes a deep breath. The air smells like cranberries. It wouldn't be Hillcrest without the tart scent of cranberry in the air.

It's Beginning to Look a Lot Like Christmas plays over the sound system. And it is. White lights twinkle in the rafters. Snowflakes flutter overhead suspended on invisible wires. Fake snow drifts line the sides of the promenade. Lampposts lead the way toward the prettiest little Christmas Village in all Wisconsin.

There was no saving the dilapidated mountain of plastic snow that served as the Christmas Village for as long as Candace can remember. In its place is a snow-covered Victorian home, surrounded by evergreen trees and furry woodland creatures.

Candy Cane Lane winds past a hot cocoa station, leading to Santa's throne at the heart of the display. There's even a faux fireplace, complete with stockings hung with care.

She glances at her clipboard and crosses off the first item on her list. Christmas Village has officially been overhauled.

As she walks toward the atrium, she sees elves stationed around the perimeter.

They wave to customers.

There are customers!

"Hey, Candace! Check out all the foot traffic," Babs calls out from Cranberry Crafts where she's worked for the past twenty years.

Candace beams. She walks faster.

Elves interact with people as they wait, just like she outlined in her twenty-part training manual.

There's a line! People are waiting in it!

The mall manager, Lars Anderson, pulls her aside. "You see all those folks?"

Candace clutches his hand and nods.

"No need to cry, dear." Magdalene Sheer, of Sheer Bliss Crystals and Healing, hands her a tissue. "What you've done here is a miracle. I never saw it coming."

With a swipe of her finger, Candace realizes there are in fact, real honest to God tears in her eyes.

The business owners are more than on board. They're pleased.

With a sniffle, she crosses off the second item on her list.

All that's left is the linchpin of this whole plan. It's time she met her Santa.

Back when she was hired she knew exactly who she would ask to be Santa Claus - her parent's oldest friend, Jack Pederson.

He has a bushy beard as white as snow.

His eyes twinkled through twenty hours of Santa training.

He knows the elves by name and every store in the mall.

His *ho ho ho*'s make his belly jiggle and leave everyone feeling like an excited kid on Christmas morning.

But just twelve hours before the opening of Christmas Village, Mr. Pederson slipped as he put up his Christmas lights. He'll be in traction until sometime after the new year.

Luckily, Dudley Knickerbocker, one of her most enthusiastic elves, said he had the perfect replacement. He called the guy a real "Santa's Santa". Candace wasn't convinced until Dudley swore on his grandfather's cranberry bog.

It doesn't get more serious than that in Hillcrest.

The town is located in Wisconsin's heartland, the cranberry capital of the world. Everyone's got a brother, uncle, or nephew working the bogs. Without those little red gems Oak Grove probably wouldn't exist.

In the fall, during harvest season, the air is heavy with the smell of cranberries. Once the harvest ends, Christmas season comes along and they're baked into pies, added to stuffing, turned into candles, and strung from evergreens. Cranberries are all anyone thinks about in Hillcrest for a solid six months out of the year.

Until this year.

This year they'll be talking about Candace's Christmas Village, too.

PART TWO

The New Santa's...Lap

Nick Frost never thought he'd be back home after leaving almost a decade ago.

He certainly never thought he'd come back to sit on a throne built for a fake North Pole or wear a hand-me-down Santa suit that's two sizes too big.

This wasn't supposed to be his life.

He's supposed to be back in Silicon Valley, making a name for himself so he could retire before sixty.

He was so close to making that dream a reality.

Now he's right back where he started, in Hillcrest, Wisconsin.

Home of the *Fighting Cranberries*.

To make things worse, he's literally perched in the middle of Oak Grove Mall for all his old school alumni to see. And mock.

The Santa suit sucks. The fat suit underneath it sucks. The pay definitely sucks.

His life…*sucks*.

Instead of schmoozing in Palo Alto, he's playing Santa to a bunch of kids who belong to old classmates who either loved this town enough to stay, or it just never crossed their minds to leave.

Nick doesn't understand either of those scenarios. In fact he doesn't understand why he took this job in the first place.

Actually, he does. It's pretty simple. And sad.

He needs money. He needs a place to stay. And he needs a do-over in the worst kind of way.

At first Nick thought he'd lucked out when an old high school buddy told him about an opening at the mall. Now he's not sure he should consider Dudley a friend at all.

He's also not sure if he'll make enough money to move out of his parents house, or if he'll end up a man-child, dependent on them for the rest of his life.

That thought alone makes his stomach churn.

It also makes him use words like asinine and idiotic when a boy asks him for the latest talking Baby Yoda plushy that's selling out like crazy.

The result is a red faced boy with a high pitched wail, and the parents of said child wearing horrified expressions.

"You'll thank me when they get pulled off the shelves because they sound less like friendly galactic space creatures and more like the exorcist," he says, hoping to convince them not to waste their money.

"Um, excuse me…*Santa*." A woman glares down at him in disapproval.

He shifts in his seat as he fakes a cough.

He should probably be concerned, but he's too busy appreciating the sparkle in her eyes, and the faint scent of cranberries that she's brought with her.

He moved over two thousand miles across the country to get away from that fragrance. Today he doesn't mind it at all.

Mrs. Jones grabs her son from Santa's lap and stomps off in a huff. "If I wanted his opinion…" she mutters to herself.

Candace is torn between rushing after them to apologize and stepping in to save a long line of kids from her rogue Santa.

He draws out a bored yawn from his throne, but his bright green eyes are intense. It's disconcerting.

He taps his foot impatiently as he waits for his next… victim?

It's not jolly.

Not one bit.

It's not the only un-Santa thing about him either.

He's pretty lean under the fat suit.

He's at least thirty years younger than Mr. Pederson.

His cheeks aren't even rosy, for goodness sakes. They're... are they sun-kissed? In Wisconsin? In *winter*?

This was Dudley's perfect Santa?

Candace is going to give that elf a good talking to.

Right after she has it out with Santa.

Because she feels her three point plan crumbling beneath her feet.

"What did you just tell Bobby Jackson?" she quietly demands.

It's clear to Nick the woman is trying to avoid a scene. So, he leans toward her, closing the gap between them and whispers, "I told his *parents* not to waste their money on that piece of-"

She presses a finger against his lips, shushing him before he can finish the sentence.

The woman's eyes narrow.

She's so serious. And kind of cute in the Santa hat.

Nick tries very hard not to smile as he mumbles through her fingers. "Crap?"

"This is a family-friendly mall, Mr. Claus. What are you thinking?"

Nick takes her hand in his and slowly lowers her finger from his lips. He doesn't let go. He's not sure why. "I'm thinking these people wouldn't mind a little *family friendly* advice?"

Candace ignores the warmth of his hand. She ignores the butterflies in her stomach.

"We didn't hire you for your advice, Santa. You're here to pose for pictures and ask kids what they want for

Christmas. I know you weren't at our training sessions, but Dudley assured me you would read the manual before you started today. There is a very clear script outlined in chapter three, on page seventy-two about the appropriate way to interact with children."

Just behind her, a child wails and Candace remembers she's surrounded by customers. The quiet argument with Santa has gained their attention. In a panic, she pulls her hand from his, and smiles bravely as she straightens her skirt.

She doesn't miss the touch of his hand. At all.

Nick blinks away her cranberry fog. As he clears his throat, he sits a little taller.

"Yeah but those scripts are more like a guideline, right?" he asks. "I mean, Santa wouldn't really want parents to spend their hard earned money on something that's gonna break in a month?"

"What Santa wants is kind of irrelevant because-" Candace glances at the small army of kids waiting for their opportunity to talk to Santa. She steps closer and whispers in Nick's ear. "Because he's not real."

He feigns a gasp, covers his mouth, and widens his eyes.

Candace folds her arms across her chest and stares him dead in the eyes. "Spare me."

Nick likes a challenge. Suddenly he'd love nothing more than to debate the existence of Santa Claus with his visitor. "But if he *was* real-"

"If he *was* real I'd like to think he'd want to make my Christmas wish come true. And that doesn't include ruining this mall's Christmas Village."

Nick stops listening after *Christmas wish*. He stops noticing the stares they're garnering. He stops hearing the impatient whines of the children in line.

He's only interested in one thing, so he leans closer. "What *does* it include?"

A shiver runs down Candace's spine.

"What does *what* include?"

"Your Christmas wish."

In a heartbeat, Candace remembers the Christmas when she had her first kiss just feet from where she's standing. It was at the edge of the old Christmas Village as *Silent Night* played over the intercom and snow fell on the glass dome overhead. It was the perfect first kiss in the perfect place and nothing has lived up to it since.

She shakes her head.

She's overtired and overworked.

She really likes Santa's eyes.

And his peppermint-scented breath.

But she definitely does not want him to kiss her. The man is practically ruining their opening day.

"You here for your pic, Candace?" someone asks.

It's James, the photographer.

She tries to focus.

She has a job to do.

"My wish includes social media coverage." Candace adjusts her Santa hat. "I'm here for my picture with you, Santa."

Nick was hoping for something a little more personal. "That's not very exciting."

"You clearly haven't been paying attention to our *exciting* marketing campaign."

He lets out a chuckle that might be construed by younger visitors as jolly. If they were being generous. "Is there such a thing as an exciting marketing campaign?"

"Follow us on Insta and you'll get your answer."

"I'll do that," he promises, bewildered.

Why doesn't he mind the smell of cranberries anymore? And what does she *really* want for Christmas?

"Hello!" A woman wrangling two toddlers calls from the front of the line. "You're holding us up, dear."

"Mind if I…" Candace nods to Nick's lap.

In theory this was supposed to be easy. Take a pic on Santa's lap and post it online. Instead, she's a ball of nerves, her traitorous body tingling from the tip of her Santa cap to the toes of her red patent leather pumps.

"Um," Nick manages to utter, barely. The truth is, he doesn't mind. He doesn't mind one bit.

"It's not for me. It's for the mall," she feels the need to explain.

"No, yeah, right, sure." Nick awkwardly adjusts his glasses, a nervous habit. Before he knows it, she's on his lap and he's fully engulfed in her cranberry perfume.

Not that he can't handle a woman on his lap but why does she have to smell so fucking good?

"You two gonna smile?" James asks from behind the lens of the camera.

It's almost like Candace needed permission. Once she lets herself go, she can't stop smiling. Her nerves give way to a fluttery feeling in her chest. She's so excited, she wraps her arms around his neck.

This Santa's not that bad.

Not bad at all.

He might just work out.

As Candace gets comfortable on Nick's lap, he forgets where he is, what he's doing, who he's supposed to be. His hand settles on Candace's hip. He breathes her in.

He relaxes a little, trying to concentrate on the camera instead of the way she leans into him.

Then his curiosity gets the better of him again.

"So, besides Insta fame, what do you really want for Christmas?"

"I want…" Candace murmurs as she stares past Santa's glasses and into his eyes. Words fail her. As the camera flashes, the things that come to mind are absolutely inappropriate. Like Santa's got strong hands. And a nice mouth.

It's all too much for Candace. She closes her eyes and takes a deep breath.

It doesn't help.

Santa smells like pine.

She sighs.

A smile tugs at the corners of Nick's lips. He can't believe he's getting hit on in this hideous outfit. "Come on, you can tell me," he urges. "I'm Santa, remember?"

He's Santa, alright. She snuggles closer.

"We could grab a drink later?"

A Santa in need of serious training. He has no idea about appropriate holiday behavior or Oak Grove's HR policies. And he's making her feel things she definitely should not be feeling at work. Santa should never do that.

Candace thought she was hitting it out of the park. She can't believe she's doing it all wrong.

When the photoshoot is over, she practically jumps off his lap.

"Come to the office later so we can go over your training manual. Santa is thirty-three percent of my plan to save this place."

Confused, Nick tries to reconcile two things:

A. He is definitely *not* getting hit on.

B. He wishes he was.

Regardless, his urge to tease her outweighs his disappointment.

"Only thirty-three? That seems low. Isn't Santa like *the embodiment* of Christmas?"

"That's the spirit, Santa. Remember you're the key to this whole thing. You'll get the hang of it. Come find me after your shift."

Candace pulls a business card out of her pocket and hands it to her wayward Santa.

She pretends not to notice when his red velvet-covered fingertips brush over hers. She pretends not to care how the contact makes her feel. Touching Santa shouldn't be a big deal. Neither should sitting on his lap. Asking her what she wants for Christmas shouldn't bring illicit thoughts to mind.

Candace has her work cut out for her if she's going to get this Santa in line.

And there's no telling what could happen if she lingers.

Before she can lose her composure… *again*, she nods politely, turns on her heel and walks back to her office.

As she leaves, Nick thinks about the way she smiled at him earlier, about her fingers against his lips, about the tone in her voice, and that damn cranberry perfume. She smells like…Christmas. And home. Two things he thought he could do without.

He peeks down at her business card and pushes his glasses up to read.

"Candace Kane."

Nick likes saying her name. He likes bantering with her, too.

But he can't get involved with someone from Hillcrest.

He's not staying.

And she's his boss.

"What is wrong with me?"

"You suck as a Santa, that's what's wrong!" an obnoxious kid yells. All his little minion friends laugh. Their parents try not to.

Nick's brow furrows. "Screw you, kid."

The child's mother gasps. People in line begin to murmur.

And okay, maybe a little training isn't a bad idea.

PART THREE

The Training

Candace's assistant knocks on her office door. "Santa's here to see you."

Candace glances up from her monitor where she was scrolling through the pics James sent over. In her favorite, she's sitting on Santa's lap with one of her pumps dangling from her toes.

She looks like she's in love.

Or in lust.

Whatever she is, it's totally inappropriate. He's her employee.

It looks like he felt it too, though. His hand clutched her thigh as he looked deep into her eyes and asked what she wanted for Christmas.

"Want me to bring him in?"

"Who?"

Jenny giggles and glances at the paperwork in her hands. "Mr., um… Frost?"

"Excuse me?"

"Big guy. Bushy beard. Velvet suit." Jenny blushes. "Nice eyes."

Right. It's time to tame, er, *train* her wayward Santa.

Candace takes another glance at her monitor. "Set him up in the conference room. And let me have a look at those documents. I'll run them to HR."

Nick has to force his foot to stop bouncing as he waits for his boss.

He feels more like he's been called to the principal's office than a friendly training session. He hasn't been this jittery since his first internship with Yahoo.

He reminds himself he's not some kid, fresh out of college. He's a mature, logical, self-sufficient adult who's meeting with another mature, logical, self-sufficient adult.

One who placed a finger against his lips and scolded him one minute then sat on his lap the next. One who looked into his eyes like she felt the same spark he did, then promptly ran away.

Well, she didn't run.

She walked.

Sashayed, really.

Like a boss.

Dammit. Nick's back to being nervous.

When Candace peeks into the conference room where Santa's waiting, she remembers Nick Frost. She had no idea he was the one underneath that red velvet suit and beard.

He was in her brother's class, but disappeared by the time she was a sophomore. She's dying to know where he's been keeping himself the last nine years. How he's gone from a scrawny mathlete to a sexy Santa.

They could cover those details after training.

Over a drink at Hennigan's.

She's got to snap out of it, though. It's not going to happen. She's holding this man's W-2's in her hand.

Candace clears her throat. Santa looks up from the table and into her eyes. She grabs hold of the door for support.

Nick sees the manual in her hands. A four inch thick manual. Clearly this isn't going to be the easy, laid back job he hoped it would be.

"Wow that's..." He's not sure what superlative would do the book justice. "I am gonna read the shit out of that later. Promise."

There's no way he's reading the entire thing.

He'll skim it. Skimming works.

Candace drops the manual in front of Nick. The table shakes on impact.

"Santa" is doodled on the front in sparkly red and green ink, along with a candy cane, and is that...a red-nosed reindeer?

Candace takes a seat across from Nick and smiles brightly. The Santa hat is gone. Long brown waves of hair frame her face perfectly and highlights match the little flecks of gold in her eyes.

She looks familiar, but he can't quite place how he knows her.

"I thought we'd go through this together. We've got to get you into tip top Santa shape as soon as possible."

"Seriously?" Nick checks his watch.

"Listen, Mr. Frost, if you don't want to be here just let me know."

Candace prays he doesn't get up and leave. A Christmas Village without Santa would be a tragedy. Her plan to save Oak Grove would be over before it even began.

Although he's tempted to, Nick knows he can't leave. He needs this job.

"No, no, I'm here for this," he tells her. "Really."

Candace sighs, relieved. "Glad to hear it. Get comfortable, Santa. You've got some training to do."

Nick removes his hat and beard. He sets them on the table as he shrugs out of his Santa jacket. He rolls his neck to relieve some of the tension that's been building all day.

He nudges his glasses up the bridge of his nose.

Candace cannot take her eyes off of him.

His bushy beard hid his defined jaw.

The velvet jacket hid the way he's filled in since high school.

And with those glasses, he looks like the hottest Christmas nerd she's ever seen.

Candace likes nerds.

She's one herself.

She has the manual to prove it.

Right.

The manual.

Nick Frost isn't sitting here to get ogled. He's here for training.

"I, um… maybe we should jump to page one-eighteen."

Candace pulls the manual in her direction and starts reading aloud. "Santa is the embodiment of the holiday season." She pauses and peeks over the edge of the manual.

"Should I come to you?" Nick points to Candace's side of the table.

"No, I think you can embody Christmas where you are."

"I'll do my best," he promises with a laugh.

Candace is certain Christmas never looked this sexy. So she goes back to hiding behind the manual.

"Santa must do his best to make guests at Oak Grove's Christmas Village feel welcome. They should leave your lap with certainty that their gift ideas are good ones, and the Oak Grove Mall is the place to make their Christmas wishes come true."

As Candace reads from the manual, Nick thinks back to having her in his arms. He'd do just about anything to see her smile like she did for the camera.

"Did you leave my lap feeling like it's the place to make your Christmas wishes come true?"

Candace's mouth drops open.

Nick is only slightly mortified he actually said those words out loud. "Sorry."

"This isn't about me, Nick," she says as much to convince herself as the man across the table from her. "It's about all the kids out there. This place can be magic when you're young. Christmas Village is just the start. This mall has so much potential. We can't just let it go."

"You really care about this place, huh?" Nick realizes. He sees it in her eyes, hears it in her voice.

Santa seems like he really cares.

"You ever just realize where you're supposed to be? What you're supposed to be doing?"

Nick remembers how excited he was to land his dream job. And how devastated he was to lose it. "I thought I had."

The melancholy in Nick's voice takes Candace by surprise.

"Then you know how important this is to me."

"Yeah, I do."

Over the next half hour, Nick learns about hidden surprises in the Christmas Village, which stores shoppers should visit, and the Candace-approved way to greet kids and their families.

Nick tries to place her.

Kane.

He tutored a guy named Christian Kane in high school. Maybe she's his cousin, or... sister?

The only thing Nick remembers about the guy is that he was passionate about football. Candace is passionate about... everything.

And she's personable. Funny.

Sexy.

Nick stops himself. He can't think about his boss being sexy.

He needs this job. The last thing he wants is–

"Nick! Hellooo in there!" Candace calls out. "Want to give it a try?"

"Absolutely!" *Wait*. "What?"

She stands and smooths her skirt.

"It's time for some role playing."

"You want to…" Nick's not sure how they went from studying to be a Santa to being part of a BDSM session.

Candace bites her bottom lip. "It's showtime, Santa."

"What now?"

"You remember your lines?" she asks, walking toward him.

"Lines?" Nick can't think of his own name much less any lines they might have discussed.

"Ho, ho ho?" Candace asks, handing him his Santa hat.

"You mean..." Nick remembers where he is, what they're doing. "Right. No, yeah, totally."

He takes the hat and sets it on his head.

The last thing Nick wants is to disappoint her. So, he swallows down the nervous energy he gets every time Candace is this close and goes for it.

"Ho, um… ho… ho?"

He feels like an idiot, and sounds *nothing* like the Santa he remembers from when he was a kid. But Nick is determined. He peeks down at the words on the paper as if he needs a refresher and tries again.

"Ho, *ho, ho*." He clears his throat. *Better.* "*Ho* ho ho."

Suddenly, an old rap song plays in his head. Run DMC used to be his favorite.

"*Yo*, ho," he says, trying to sound *hip,* or *lit,* maybe is the better word this year. But he knows, immediately, it was a bad idea. Nick is neither of those things. Never has been. Never will be.

"Maybe not that last one."

Candace tries her best not to laugh.

Her smile is infectious. Nick stifles a laugh of his own. He focuses on the words in front of him instead of the cranberry scent that keeps tempting him to bury his nose into her neck and breathe her in until he's had his fill.

Next line, he thinks, then searches for his spot in the script.

"Err, what's your name, *little boy or girl*?" he asks, repeating exactly what's in front of him.

Candace rolls her eyes. "I'm a girl, Nick."

The playful look she's giving him makes him speak without thinking. "Yeah you are."

Candace isn't sure if Nick's being sarcastic, flirty, or observant. She decides observant is the safest option. "You probably want to decide if they're a boy or girl before you greet them."

"I don't know, maybe you should revise this book. What if they don't identify with either?"

Candace plucks the manual out of Nick's hands and strikes the boy or girl line. He's annoying but he's got a point.

"Happy?" she asks as she hands it back to him.

"Very."

Nick smiles.

Not because Candace just admitted he was right. Because she's clearly flustered and he's letting himself believe, for just a second or two, that it's him who's doing that to her.

"Wonderful. Now let's pick up where we left off."

"Right… um.." Nick slides a finger across the page to find his spot. "Do you… want to come sit on my lap and tell me what you want for Christmas, *insert name here*?"

"Oh my goodness, you know my name."

He's making this difficult. He's absolutely frustrating. Even so, she can't think of anything else she wants more than to sit on this man's lap.

Nick could interrogate her about why the line would be in the book if Santa is supposed to know all of this already.

But he'd much rather say her name.

"Candace."

He imagines another question he'd like to ask instead of the line in his manual. A question that might find them having dinner and drinks later.

It's a question he definitely shouldn't ask again.

"Would you like to come sit on my lap and tell me what you want for Christmas?"

When Nick says her name and looks into her eyes, Candace doesn't give it a second thought. Before he can push the chair away from the table she slides onto his lap like it was made for her. Wedged between Nick and the table, her heart beats a mile a minute.

Candace never had a thing for Santa.

Nick never wanted to *be* Santa.

Until today.

Jenny pokes her head into the conference room. Her jaw drops when she finds her boss on Nick's lap. "I was gonna head home but um, want me to stick around?"

Candace looks from Jenny to Nick. Her mouth goes dry. "No, I've got this," she says looking into Santa's eyes.

They're deep, forest green, like the grove of cedars behind her parents' house.

"Oookay. See you tomorrow, boss."

The conference door swings shut.

Lights flick off in the hallway.

They're officially alone.

"How um…" Nick tries desperately to think straight. But who is he kidding? With Candace on his lap, thinking has officially gone out the window.

Nick blinks. He tries to remember what line comes next. "Age." Then he attempts to sound more like Santa, and less like a caveman.

"I mean, how old are you, little… *you*?" He catches himself at the last second. Candace is no child.

Sitting this close to Nick, Candace has to think hard to come up with the right answer.

"I'm, um, twenty-four."

Nick does the math quickly. He's only three years older.

He wonders if they ever sat in the same movie theater, or played at the same arcade?

Did they ever cross paths in high school?

"Did you grow up here?" he asks without another thought.

"Excuse me, but that's not in the manual. Also, it's something Santa should definitely know."

"Do you always avoid answering questions, Candace?"

"Do you want to be here all night, Nick?"

He'd stay forever if she asked. Part of him knows that's not what she meant. The other part wishes she did.

"Right," he clears his throat. "Moving on. Favorite part about Christmas?"

He looks at her like he really wants to know.

The first thing that comes to Candace's mind is, "You," but that wouldn't make any sense. Even though his breath smells like peppermint and his voice sounds like velvet. They just met. He can't be her favorite thing about this holiday.

"Hillcrest, I guess," she admits. "And this mall. It wouldn't feel like Christmas anywhere else. What about you, Nick?"

When she says his name she feels his entire body tense. Now *she's* the one going off script. "I mean… Santa."

"I… wait, that's…" He tears his eyes away from hers. He double-checks the manual. He reads ahead. Finally, he gives up. "Are you trying to trip me up?"

"Oh, um, right. Sorry." Candace is strangely disappointed.

She really wants to know if Nick likes sledding down the hill behind Jensen's farm. Does he like the spiked hot cocoa they make at Donna's Delights? His eyes aren't giving anything away. Or his chest. Or his biceps.

Candace needs to concentrate.

"Forgiven," he says with a playful grin. "But only because I hear you've been very good this year."

Candace gazes into Nick's eyes. "Think so?" she whispers.

He's only known her for less than a day, but he can feel it in his bones. Candace is good, through and through.

"Not a doubt in my mind."

"You're not so bad yourself, Santa." She wraps her arms around his neck.

Nick's eyes dip to watch Candace lick her lips. She tilts her head.

She's so close.

He can barely breathe.

Until *Mother Lovin' Mother* starts playing on his phone, somewhere inside his Santa suit. Then he pretty much wants to die.

Candace jumps off Nick's lap. The training manual slams onto her foot and she yelps as she limps to the other end of the conference room.

Nick's face is on fire as he answers his phone.

"Mom, what's up?" he asks, watching Candace straighten her skirt.

"Hi, honey. I"m sorry to bother you at work, I just wanted to make sure you remember to stop and get the eggs and milk for me on your way home."

He closes his eyes. He could be a forty year old man and still feel fifteen when his mother calls.

"The sticky note you left me this morning is still in the car, Mom."

"Oh, good. Can you also see if they have any of those chocolate covered pretzels your father loves?"

Nick makes eye contact with Candace as she rubs her sore foot. If only he could magically erase her memory of this moment.

"Yep."

"And some toilet paper."

Awesome. "Got it mom, I gotta-"

"Do you have enough money for gas?"

Nick sighs before lying to his mother. "I'm good, Mom. No gas money needed."

Candace looks very busy at the other end of the conference table.

"You're such a sweet boy," Nicks's mother coos.

If she only knew what he was hoping to do a few seconds before she called. "Oooh-kay, Mom. Gotta go."

"I'll see you soon, dear."

"Yep."

"I love you."

Fuck. Why did she have to throw out the L-bomb?

Nick can't *not* say it back. But he can't have Candace hear him tell his mommy he loves her, like a twelve year old boy going away to sleep over camp for the first time, either.

He decides to go with a whisper. "Love you too."

"I'm sorry, honey, what?"

He mumbles a little louder. "I love you too, Mom."

And it's official. Anything that might have been happening between him and Candace has died a sad death.

"Okay, dear. See you soon."

He presses *end*, slips the phone back into his pocket, and grimaces.

Candace tucks some papers into a folder. "You know, if you need gas money I can expedite this paperwork. Get you on the payroll in time for next Friday."

Nick might die from embarrassment after all.

"Nope. I am… all good," he tries to convince her.

Candace decides she's going to do it anyway.

"So, I'm gonna… go, if that's cool with you? I have a lot of *groceries* to pick up, apparently."

"Jensen's has milk on sale this week," Candace offers.

He said he had gas money. He made no claims about milk money.

"Right. Thanks." Nick grabs his things and makes a mad dash for the conference room door just as his phone rings again.

He immediately regrets answering it.

"No, Mom, I did not hang up on you…"

Before Candace can process what just happened, she spots Nick's training manual laying on the floor. Milk money or not, Santa still has some studying to do.

"Nick!" she calls.

But Santa's too busy talking to his mom to hear.

PART FOUR

The Locker Room

Nick takes full advantage of the employee locker room. This Santa suit has been suffocating him since the start of his training session. He can't get out of it fast enough.

When he first put it on, he was swimming in it. Now it feels like he's peeling shrink wrap off of a potato, for Christ's sake.

The hat is easy, the boots, not so much. He struggles with the suspenders, but he finally declares victory and shoves the rest of his outfit off in one fell swoop.

In his boxer briefs, and nothing but his boxer briefs, Nick tilts his head back, closes his eyes, and falls against the lockers. He lets out a long, heavy sigh of relief.

"Get her out of your head, Nick. She's not gonna make out with you. Certainly not in a Santa suit. *Idiot.*"

And stop imagining her cranberry perfume.

He takes a deep breath, tries to clear his head. But he can almost feel her arms around him. And he can almost hear her calling his name.

"Nick? Nick, are you in here?"

"Shit."

He's not imagining her voice. That *is* her voice. And the sound of her heels on the tile floor.

"Oh my God."

"Oh my God!"

Candace covers her eyes with Nick's enormous training manual.

Nick grabs the closest thing he can find to cover his...

Immediately, he realizes, what he thought was his Santa jacket, is actually his Santa *hat* and it is not doing a very good job of covering *any* part of him whatsoever, much less the one thing he should definitely not be exposing to Candace.

"I'm so sorry!" he blurts out, trying not to look at her as he fumbles to find something to throw over himself.

"No! I'm sorry. I shouldn't even be here. I didn't think–. I, um... you left this."

Candace covers her eyes as she holds the manual in Nick's general direction. After what feels like forever, she peeks through her fingers. Nick's frozen against the lockers, with his Santa hat over his...

She should not be looking.

She *needs* to stop looking.

Because all he's wearing are black boxer briefs and glasses.

Nick feigns a cough, unsure what to do.

Candace spins so she's facing the wall. She slowly walks backward toward the nearest bench where she can safely place the manual. The heel of her pump gets caught on something red and velvet. The next thing she knows a big black belt is looped around her ankle and she's going down.

"Gotcha," Nick breathes, catching Candace before she can hit the floor.

As he looks down at her in his arms, his glasses slide to the tip of his nose. It's all she can do not to push them back up for him.

"Thanks."

"My pleasure."

He holds onto her a little longer than he has to. Definitely longer than he should.

She's your boss. She's your boss. She's your boss.

"Most of the guys just leave their wallet and their car keys in their lockers. I think. I mean, I don't check. Ever. So I could be wrong on this."

"Candace?"

"Yes, Nick?"

"That's not my wallet."

Candace bolts to the other side of the locker room. She looks everywhere except at Nick's *wallet*. Her face is the color of Nick's Santa suit.

He grabs his Levis as Candace heads for the exit.

"So, do you always work this late?" he asks, stepping into his jeans.

"Usually," she replies, reaching for the door.

"Why here?"

"It's my job, Nick."

It's not the first time someone's asked her this question.

It's the first time she wishes she answered differently.

It's enough to make her pause.

Nick grabs a shirt out of his backpack and pulls it over his head. "You're fucking talented, and smart is all I'm saying. Why not San Francisco? Or even Irvine Spectrum, they would both be lucky to have you."

"There are tons of people dying to work there. They don't need me. And Hillcrest is home."

He finds his Tevas in his backpack and curses.

"Everything ok back there?" she asks.

"Not exactly." He scowls at his sandals.

"Is it safe for me to...?" When Candace doesn't finish, Nick peeks over to see her whirling her hand in the air, making a circular motion.

He takes a moment to chuckle silently. "Absolutely. All clear."

When she turns around she finds him barefoot in jeans and a T-shirt, holding a pair of sandals in his hand.

"What in the world are those?"

"These," he glares at them. "Are *not* winter shoes."

"You could always wear your Santa boots home."

Nick eyes the monstrosities laying on the ground and sighs as he shoves the Tevas back into his bag.

Candace giggles. Then remembers she's standing in the employee locker room. She makes a mental note to report herself to HR in the morning.

"I'm sorry. About laughing. About barging in. About…"

"Hey, it's your mall. I'm the one who probably should have waited until I got home to change."

"I just hope I didn't scare you off."

"Me?" He scoffs. "Scared? Pfffft."

She laughs. She's blushing. It's gorgeous.

"Just promise me you'll come back tomorrow? I wouldn't want those ninety minutes of training to go to waste."

Right.

Those ninety minutes.

Of embarrassment, amusement, and ultimately... enjoyment.

Of getting to know his new boss. Then nearly kissing that boss in a split second terrible decision because he could get fired for doing it.

Ninety minutes he wouldn't take back for all the money in Silicon Valley.

Because bad decisions aside, Nick just spent the last ninety minutes *not* thinking about all the shitty things that happened to him before having to come home with his tail tucked between his legs.

Thanks to Candace.

"I promise," he tells her.

She smiles. "Thanks, Santa. Night."

She sneaks one more look over her shoulder before she slips out of the locker room.

"Night." Nick whispers, unexpectedly looking forward to being Santa tomorrow.

PART FIVE

Home Sweet Home

On the drive home, Nick realizes he's smiled more today than he has in months.

"Candace Kane."

He makes a note to look her up when he gets back to his parent's house. He's sure they still have his old yearbooks somewhere.

"Hi, honey. How'd it go?" Nick's mother asks when he steps inside his childhood home. "Did you get the-"

He plops the grocery bag onto the counter and warms his hands over the stove. "I forgot how fucking cold it is here."

His mother gives him a look.

"Sorry." Nick feels like he's seventeen again. Like he's trapped. Again.

He starts toward his temporary basement bedroom.

"Isn't Candace great?"

Her question stops him short.

Nick's lips lift at the edges. "She is, actually."

"I think she's *sinnnngle*!"

"Leave him alone, Margret!" His dad yells from his La-Z-Boy in the living room. The TV plays *Home Improvement* in the background. If Nick didn't know any better, he'd assume his dad hadn't moved from that spot in almost ten years.

Nick's mother unloads her groceries. "Jonathon Frost, it is a mother's duty to push her children to make good choices in life and Candace is the best choice Nick could ever make."

"She's my boss, you know that right?" Nick reminds his mother. Or maybe himself.

She slaps his arm. "Boss, schmoss. She's adorable."

Nick is *not* having this conversation with his mother. Not right now, anyway. "I'm going to bed."

"Sure honey. I'll make you a good breakfast in the morning. Want some apple and cinnamon oatmeal?"

Nick scowls. He's not twelve.

"How about Cream of Wheat instead?"

He hangs his head, defeated.

"And I'll pack you a ham and cheese tomorrow. You used to *love* ham and cheese sandwiches. Remember? I bought the good stuff this week. Boar's Head."

Nick does love Boar's Head.

No.

No.

No.

She can pack him all the sandwiches she wants. But Nick is not taking lunch to the mall tomorrow. The last thing he needs is for Candace to think he can't fend for himself.

"Not necessary, Mom."

She's still planning out his next five meals as Nick heads downstairs and takes a shower.

Once he's done, he finds his high school yearbooks buried in a closet. They're in an old trunk labeled "Nicky".

He starts with senior year, flipping through a few pages. Chris Kane's face is plastered all over the place. He was football captain, most popular, best bud to the cheerleaders, prankster, and in one random classroom, sitting in a chair, he even looks... studious.

Another boy's back is to the camera. No one else would ever know it was Nick in that photo, helping Chris pass math so he could stay on the team.

Nick remembers, though. Like it was yesterday.

He remembers how grateful Chris was when he finally understood compound equations. He remembers Chris's teammates giving him hell about needing a tutor. He remembers acting like he didn't hear any of it, so Chris wouldn't feel like an idiot after they were gone. And he remembers Chris thanking him profusely after passing his exam with a B.

Nick flips through a few more pages and stops as soon as he sees her, standing next to Chris with a bunch of other people. After a game maybe.

He'd know *that* smile anywhere.

He doesn't even realize how hard he's smiling until his jaw aches.

He flips back to the freshman section and finds Candace again. It's a much better picture of her. Close up. Eyes bright, smiling huge for the camera, much like earlier.

Her hair was longer then, lighter. She looks so young in this photo.

"I'm in big trouble."

Even as he warns himself to be careful with his new boss, Nick remembers he promised Candace he'd follow her on Insta.

So he pulls his phone out and searches for the Oak Grove Mall account.

Eventually, he finds it.

@BestMallinAmericranberries

Of course.

He scrolls through the pics of each store and their owners. Candace probably took these photos. And she probably took the time to add a special individualized write up for each of them.

He sees she's liked all the posts with another account. He clicks her name. And grins.

UW Class of '20 & '22

Cheesehead forever.

Living life. Loving cranberries.

Catch me at @BestMallinAmericranberries

She's posted the first snow of the year on Main Street, the cranberry harvest at her uncle's bog, pics of workers assembling Christmas Village, an idea board for Christmas decorations.

Before he forgets, he clicks back to the mall's account and taps *follow*.

Before he loses his nerve, he follows Candace, too.

As he scrolls through her posts, he reads the comments.

@CandaceKane we're so proud of you!

@CandaceKane is the best thing that ever happened to Oak Grove Mall!

@CandaceKane thanks for caring <3

He stops when he gets to a post with multiple photos. It's titled, "THE PLAN".

Interested, Nick swipes.

The first pic is an older version of the Christmas Village he remembers from when he was a kid. It pales in comparison to what Candace has done. A red, swirly font on top, reads, "Overhaul Christmas Village".

Nick swipes again. People are hanging decorations in their stores. Over top of this one is a bolder font that says, "Get the business owners on board".

His smile widens. Of course this is Candace's doing.

He swipes again and there's a picture of Santa's throne, empty and old. The fabric looks worn, the lighting sucks. The words overtop of this photo make his stomach churn.

"Hire the best Santa the Oak Grove Mall has ever seen".

The best Santa?

The *best* Santa?

"She really got the wrong guy," he says to an empty room.

PART SIX

Santa's Lap Take Two

"You've got to be kidding, Aunt Candace."

Mackenzie bats at the sparkling, dinner plate sized snowflakes hanging in front of her face and peers at the long line snaking almost to the food court. Candace notices it's a lot longer than it was yesterday despite Santa's attitude.

"I *definitely* don't have time for this. I…I think I have soccer practice."

Candace narrows her eyes. Her niece may be wily, but she's only eight. "And here I thought the state championship was two weeks ago. I must have been dreaming when I brought your team to celebrate at Baskin Robbins."

Candace was not dreaming. She knows this for a fact because Ray, the assistant manager at Baskin Robbins, has been asking her out ever since.

"Is that Taylor's *mom* on Santa's lap?" Mackenzie asks, interrupting Candace' thoughts as they shuffle around the corner and Santa's throne comes into view.

Candace's mouth drops open.

Yes it is. Cathay Olsen's arms are wrapped around Santa's neck just like Candace's were yesterday.

Candace takes a closer look at the line. Half the people don't even have kids with them.

"What in the world?" she wonders out loud.

"Does Santa even bring grown-ups gifts?" Mackenzie asks.

The way Cathy cuddles up to Nick, it's obvious what kind of gifts she's after. The same kind Candace was dreaming about as she tossed and turned in bed.

"Like, I thought he just brings gifts to good boys and girls. Is Taylor's mom good?"

"Doesn't look like it," Candace mutters as she watches the woman rub the toe of her boot up the back of Santa's calf.

Martha Bloomfield passes Candace, pulling her daughter along with her as they leave Christmas Village. "*Love* the new Santa, Candace! Genius!"

"I didn't even get to tell him what I wanted," her daughter whines.

"Shush, we're late." Martha hisses as they rush off.

"This Santa seems pretty weird, Aunt Candace."

"He's no Mr. Pederson," Candace replies.

"Not even close," Mackenzie agrees.

As Cathy Olsen ends her whispered conversation with Nick, he notices Candace standing in line, holding a little girl's hand.

He coughs purposefully, and puts some space between himself and Cathy.

"Ho Ho Ho! Sorry about that!" he says in his best attempt at a jolly voice.

Mackenzie doesn't look convinced. "You're a very strange Santa Claus."

Nick tries to stay in character. "That's because I'm not from the North Pole like most of my Santa siblings."

"Wait. Does Santa even have siblings? I thought he just had elves. In the *North Pole*."

He peeks over at Candace who simply lifts an eyebrow.

"It's…. literally impossible for there to only be *one* Santa, little girl," he informs her, unable to help himself. "There are lots of Santas in lots of malls all around the world."

Nick's proud of himself for coming up with a great bit on such short notice.

Candace motions to an imaginary training manual in her hands, reminding him to *stick to the script.*

Mackenzie steps up to Nick, goes up on tiptoe and whispers into his ear, "I don't think you're supposed to say that."

He whispers back, "Don't get me fired in front of your… mom?"

"Where?" Mackenzie scans the crowd.

"Um, anyway... what do you want for Christmas this year?" he asks with a deeper voice than Candace remembers him having.

"That's easy. The iPhone 17XL. Mom says I'm too little. But I *need* it, Santa. *If* that's your real name."

Nick's jaw clenches. He's not a fan of iPhones. So when he notices Candace paying attention to another customer, he takes the opportunity to warn the little girl.

"Between you and me, you don't want the iPhone."

"But I really do."

"You sure you don't want to think about the new Android?"

Mackenzie scrunches up her face like she just sucked on a lemon. "Ew. Why?"

Just like that he's no longer Santa. He's Nick Frost, tech geek. "It's cheaper for one. But aside from that it's a lot more versatile."

"What's *versatile*?"

"It means you can use it for a lot of different things besides just texting your friends"

"I'm eight. Why do I need to do something besides texting?"

He pulls his Android out and shows her. "Um, pinned icons? Widgets on the home page, the *back* button? Don't even get me started on the volume control. Plus you can expand your memory without buying one of those stupid fu...dging expander packs."

"Are you sure Aunt Candace really hired you?"

"Sort of," he says. "I mean, yeah, technically."

"You're technically a really weird Santa."

Nick smiles, proud. "Thanks, kid."

"She's not wrong," Candace says.

Nick fumbles with his phone but manages to put it away.

"Everyone smile!" the photographer hollers.

Mackenzie hops onto Nick's lap. He wraps his arm around Candace's waist and pulls her in close. It feels right.

Nick's smile is genuine as he watches Candace, watching her niece. His boss looks thoughtful. He wonders what's on her mind. He'd ask, but that would entail going off script.

They can't have that.

The flash goes off and Mackenzie hops up to leave. Dudley hands her a candy cane. "Merry Christmas!"

"Dudley!" Nick hopes he's discreet.

"Yes, *Santa*?" Dudley replies, reminding Nick who he's supposed to be.

Nick couldn't care less.

He impatiently holds his hand out. "Gimme a candy cane."

Dudley scowls. "You're not supposed to-"

"Just give me the god d- ang candy cane, *my little elf.*" He smiles for the crowd.

Dudley slaps one into Nick's hand, begrudgingly, and Nick runs after Candace. She freezes when she sees Santa charging after her.

He smiles wide as he hands her the treat. "A candy cane for Candy K-"

"Don't even say it, Santa."

She hates that nickname.

And Nick's gone way off script. He's not acting like Santa at all. Since when has Santa flirted with moms? Since when does he run after mall employees?

And how did he even get a candy cane? That's Dudley's job.

Candace needs to tell Nick this is all unacceptable. Instead she feels her cheeks going warm and the corners of her mouth tipping up in a smile.

"Have you figured out what you really want for Christmas yet?" Nick asks with a wink.

Candace sighs. "We've been over this."

"Come on Candace, there's gotta be something other than social media popularity."

"I want…" Candace looks him over, from the white pom pom on the tip of his hat, to his shiny black boots. The word "you" almost pops out of her mouth again, for the second time in as many days. "I want the businesses here to turn a profit. It's my job, Santa."

"Okay," he says. He leaves out that he doesn't believe for a second it's all she wants. Instead, he promises her, "We'll work on that."

Candace worries she's going to slip and admit what's on her mind if Nick keeps asking.

She's also worried about leaving Nick to the wolves… err moms. She turns to face the line and clears her throat. "Listen ladies, we've got to respect Santa, okay? No means no."

Women giggle. A couple leave the line, disappointed.

"I mean, I don't mind," Nick whispers to Candace. "If it's what's best for business, right?"

Candace worries she's created a monster. She tries not to worry about the bile in the back of her throat. "Just remember this is a family-friendly mall, Nick."

"Hey, *family friendly* is my new middle name," he assures her with a playful wink.

"I guess I didn't expect them to want..." Candace glances from Nick's lap to his face. Who is she kidding? She can't blame them.

"Want what?"

"Nevermind," Candace grumbles. Her niece waves goodbye to Nick *'Family-Friendly'* Frost as Trisha Ericson climbs astride his lap.

"Oh, that's not necessary. I don't take tips," he says as Trisha tries to give him a dollar bill.

"Meet me in my office. End of shift."

Nick salutes his boss. "Yes ma'am."

There's a collective "Ooooooooooh," from the women in line.

"Was Santa bad, Mommy?" Candace hears a little boy ask.

"So bad," his mom replies.

PART SEVEN

After Dark

Candace checks the clock for the tenth time in as many minutes. Nick is late but she's not surprised. There's been a line for his lap all afternoon. Everyone's talking about it.

And winking.

And snickering.

And whispering about how they'll be back tomorrow.

Candace might have to impose a lap limit.

When he finally shows up, he looks… *chipper* as he wraps his knuckles on Candace's door. "You wanted to see me?"

"What do you think you're doing out there, Nick?"

His face falls. Candace doesn't look as excited as he feels. "Um."

"You're supposed to let *kids* sit on your lap. Did the training manual say anything at all about moms?"

Nick tries to remember what the manual said about who can and who can't sit on Santa's lap.

"It didn't *not* say anything about moms."

Candace feels her blood pressure rising. "You didn't even finish reading it. Did you?"

"That's not true, I read another hundred pages." After he finished stalking her on Instagram.

"That's not even half!"

"Santa needed sleep," he says, trying to lighten the mood, but he quickly realizes Candace is not amused. "I meant to start again this morning, but I was running late, and Mom made this huge fucking breakfast I couldn't exactly say no to, and then Dad wanted to warn me about the clutch on his Civic which - hello, news flash, I already knew about."

Candace remembers Nick's call with his mother last night. She knows Mrs. Frost. She's seen her at the deli counter at Jensen's and buying candles at Cranberry Cove. Nick's father owns Frost Contracting. They fixed her dad's barn roof.

Why is she being such a hard ass with their son?

It's *not* because she's jealous.

"Who gave those women the idea your lap was open for business? Right in the middle of the mall? In the middle of the day?"

Nick's brow knits. "Why does that question sound more like an accusation?"

"Because none of this was in the training manual. This wasn't my idea."

"The training manual again." Nick throws his hands up. "So what are you saying? You think I *asked* all those women to sit on my lap? You think I just have *all* the women sitting on my lap all day every day?"

Candace doesn't want to think about that.

"What you do on your own time is your business. But when you're at the Oak Grove Mall, I have a say in who sits on your lap."

"Even if that means the customer is wrong?" Nick asks abruptly.

He hadn't expected to raise his voice, but he hadn't expected Candace's anger over the increased foot traffic, either.

Candace grits her teeth and folds her arms across her chest. The customer is *never* wrong. It's the first thing they teach you in hospitality management. *Nick* is wrong... and so right at the same time. Which is clearly the reason every woman between the age of eighteen and eighty is clambering to sit on his lap.

But this PG-13 version of Christmas Village is going to keep parents from bringing their kids.

Unless…

Unless it happens after the kids are in bed.

What if they marketed Nick to the moms on Friday and Saturday nights between now and Christmas?

Candace pulls up a spreadsheet and starts making some calculations.

Jim Johnson was just talking about letting his liquor license lapse since he didn't have much need for it during the day.

Karen Casey had started hiding adult gifts at the back of the store.

This just might work.

"Listen, we can't have ladies sitting on your lap all day long. But what about all *night* long? Friday and Saturday nights, to be specific."

"I'm not that kind of Santa, Candace," Nick tells her. He's not the type of guy to sell himself for profit.

Unless that profit would help him get out of Hillcrest and get his life back.

The thought alone is tempting. The look of unabashed hope on Candace's face makes it even more so. "How much would it pay?"

"Time and a half?"

Nick calculates how much quicker the extra money could get him out of his parent's house and back to Silicon Valley.

"Done."

"Great!" Candace chirps. She's sure she can find elves willing to work overtime. According to her spreadsheet this has huge upside potential. It's something completely new for Hillcrest - a town that hasn't seen anything new in a decade.

She should be overjoyed.

She should be as enthusiastic as the Santa Claus standing in front of her.

Dudley called Nick a real Santa's Santa, but he was wrong.

He's everyone's Santa.

She's not sure why she wants to keep everyone's Santa all to herself.

Later that night, Candace sits at her parents' kitchen table as she scrolls through her spreadsheet for the umpteenth time. She's got less than a week to plan for CVAD, otherwise known as Christmas Village After Dark.

Hillcrest holiday festivities for the twenty-one and over set will include boozy holiday drinks, seductive holiday gifts, classic holiday films, and of course... Nick.

If it weren't for him, none of this would be happening.

She should feel glad... *right*?

The Instagram ad she posted after meeting with Nick had three hundred likes before she even left the office. Those are monumental numbers for Hillcrest. Crazy, viral numbers if we're talking about the mall in particular.

Which she is.

She's dedicated her career to saving the mall.

She's been working on creating buzz for the past five months.

Now she's actually doing it.

She pulls out her phone and scrolls through Insta to prove her point. A picture of Mary Johnson sitting on Nick's lap and gazing into his eyes stares back at her. It's up to three-hundred and ninety-seven likes. The comments are... *enthusiastic*, to say the least.

Candace goes over the rules she's put in place as she pours herself another cup of coffee, just as a pair of headlights swing into the driveway.

Her big brother Christian gently closes the car door, then sees the kitchen light and heads toward the house.

"Coffee? At midnight?" he asks.

Candace collapses against the countertop, warming her hands on the mug. "There aren't enough hours. You know?"

Christian rubs the back of his neck. "Can't argue with that. I've been working around the clock to save enough for that new iPhone Mack wants. Then tonight she told Jess she doesn't want it after all. Weird."

"Weird," she agrees.

As weird as her new Santa.

"Whatcha workin' on?"

He goes for her laptop, but she leaps for it and pulls it from his hands.

"It's something new. Christmas Village for grown-ups."

Christian chuckles. "Yeah, Jess said something about that. Got us tickets for Friday night after talking to Mary."

"Mary Johnson?"

"Yeah. Who knew you had this kinda power, huh?"

"Like administrative power? At the mall?"

"Um, no." Christian pulls out his phone, taps on the screen a few times, then hands it over to her.

"You follow the mall?"

"That's not the point, you ninny."

Candace gazes at the picture of her sitting on Nick's lap and feels warm all over. She's pretty sure it's not coffee. It's an electric kind of warmth. Soft as velvet. Strong as his hand as he clutched her knee.

"I don't get it," she mumbles. She might be talking to her brother. Or maybe she's talking to herself.

"Surprised to see the guy back here. Thought he was heading to California for good."

"Really?"

"He hated everything about this place." Chris raises an eyebrow as he looks from the phone to Candace. "Not anymore, I guess."

"What do you mean?"

"Jess' friends all want a piece of whatever the two of you have going on."

"We don't have anything going on."

"Keep telling yourself that, kid."

PART EIGHT

Santa's Lap Take 3

There's a line around the block the first Friday Oak Grove Mall is open after dark.

Nick is convinced he'll need a drink or two before he finds his comfort zone. Candace is sure every Hillcrest resident over the age of twenty-one is in line.

Nick is spot on about the drinks. Candace is wrong, though, because even more people line up on Saturday.

When they're featured in the Valley Sentinel, Candace stops pretending this is a Hillcrest crowd. People are coming from all across the valley.

To drink spiked hot chocolate.

To watch old Christmas movies.

To shop for scented candles, body oil, and lingerie.

And to sit on Nick's lap.

Something he doesn't seem to mind. *At all*. Not that Candace cares.

They've kept it professional since they met in her office last week.

Nick's been the epitome of a decent Santa. He's been on time every day, he's been damn near cheerful, and he's kept to the manual. *Mostly*.

Whenever Candace hears a rumor about Nick suggesting alternative Christmas gift ideas she simply sends him a note:

Stick to the manual

In red and green sparkly ink.

Luckily, everyone else working at Christmas Village takes their training seriously. There's no reason for Candace to visit very often. No reason to watch him entertain her old high school friends… on his lap.

Nick talks himself out of a hundred reasons to stop by and see Candace, daily.

Asking if his paycheck is ready, wondering if she could double-check his hours. Requesting an extra half hour for lunch to pick up some pickles for his mother once or twice.

He certainly doesn't need to search her out whenever he gets a note from her. No matter how adorable he thinks she is. It. How adorable *it* is.

He doesn't have any opinion about the assistant manager at Baskin Robbins, Ray, talking to her more than necessary.

He definitely doesn't miss her cranberry perfume.

He hates cranberries. Doesn't he?

"I'd like to file a complaint, Santa," a woman climbing onto his lap purrs.

She may have a different shade of hair than the last. She might be taller, or more dressed up. He couldn't say. They're all starting to blur together to be honest.

"Complaint?"

She whispers into his ear. "They need to make every night an After Dark night."

If Nick were to close his eyes, he thinks he could pretend it's Candace on his lap, whispering in his ear, waiting all week to sit with him.

"Attention Oak Grove shoppers," a voice over the loudspeaker system interrupts his thoughts. "The snow we expected tonight has turned into a full blown blizzard. We're gonna have to close the festivities down in about a half hour. Sorry Santa."

"See? Made it snow, too," Nick mutters.

"Snow, and..." She looks pleasantly surprised. "What's that in your pocket Santa?"

It's the tiny liquor bottles he snagged from the bar earlier. He's pretty sure that's not the answer she's looking for. But in all honesty, if it was his dick, she'd know.

"Liquid courage?" he jokes.

"Is that what Santa's calling it these days?" The woman snuggles closer.

When Candace spots Mary Johnson practically mauling Nick on his throne, she heads straight for security.

Enough is enough.

At her insistence, two guards make a beeline for Nick, who, in a panic, bolts out of his throne. Mary trips and stumbles off of his lap. He lunges to keep her from falling and pitches forward, practically diving down the steps that lead to Candy Cane Lane.

Women in line think Nick is paying them a special visit and clamber toward him. Security tries to fend them off, but ladies still manage to pull at his coat and grab for his hat. In the chaos several small bottles of liquor spill from Nick's pockets.

He tries to pick them up as fast as he can but it's too late.

"In. My. Office," Candace commands before she turns toward the crowd. "Sorry everyone. Christmas Village is closed due to the…" Candace looks over her inebriated Santa. "the *storm*. Get home safe."

Nick was *just* craving Candace's attention. Now he isn't looking forward to discussing much of anything at all.

There's no skip in his step as he follows her to her office. No excitement about the turn out as she closes the door behind them.

There's no wondering about how she feels when she turns to face him.

He knows she's angry.

Candace takes a deep, frustrated breath.

"Are you drunk?"

"Definitely not."

"You were drinking on the job."

Nick laughs. "How could I *not* be?"

Exasperated, Candace collapses into her office chair. "Because you need to be sober at work, Nick."

"Pretty sure the manual doesn't cover women throwing themselves at my *dick*, Candace," Nick dead pans.

"Pretty sure the manual doesn't mention flirting, or leading women on, or, or… whatever performance you're putting on out there."

"Riiiiiight," he nods dramatically. "Woman magnet, right here!"

He grabs his fat suit belly and jiggles it.

"Please, you've been using that suit to your advantage from the first time we met."

"Explain how using a fucking Santa suit works to my advantage. Because in my world, this…" Nick waves a hand from the top of his Santa hat to the bottom of his shiny black boots, "…is the exact opposite of sexy."

"Are you serious right now? I literally have photographic proof." Candace holds her phone under his nose. "Deny it."

Nick jerks his head back and adjusts his glasses.

Candace is sure he's taunting her.

The fucker.

"Deny what?" he asks. "You *literally* made me do this."

"I did not make you do Mary Johnson! And I did not make you drink at work. And I…"

"Do?" Nick lets what she's said sink in. "Like… *do* Mary Johnson? Candace, I didn't *do* anyone." Nick isn't sure if he's more frustrated with himself or Candace. "If anyone was doing anyone, it was you who was … doing… talking to that Ray guy."

"It's my job, Nick. I don't flirt on the job. I don't *drink* on the job."

"And it's my job to let grown ass women sit on my lap after dark, remember? It doesn't mean I want them to. It doesn't mean I'm flirting. It certainly doesn't mean I'm *doing* them."

Candace rolls her eyes. "Wow, it must be so hard having women throw themselves at you."

"It is hard, Candace. Every woman out there wants a piece of me, except for-"

You.

Nick stops himself before crossing that line again.

Candace narrows her eyes. "Mrs. Anderson has been waiting until Christmas Eve to sit on your lap."

Nick huffs. He pulls his Santa hat off as he runs a hand through his hair. "Of course, you'd think I was talking about someone else."

"I'm talking about the drinking, Nick. I could fire you for cause."

The thought of it makes Candace sick to her stomach.

"Then why don't you?" he challenges. "Put us both out of our misery."

Nick doesn't want to quit being Santa.

What he wants is to sweep everything off of her desk, pull her out of that chair, and work through their problems in a much more productive way.

Naked.

It's killing him.

She's killing him.

She has been since the first day they met.

"Fine. You're fired."

Yep. She keeps killing him over and over again.

"Great. I hate this fucking job anyway."

He pulls his fake beard off and tosses it onto her desk, then starts unbuttoning his jacket.

"You were never any good at it."

"I was better than your other Santa." He stops fiddling with his buttons, momentarily. "Oh wait, you didn't have one."

Nick throws the jacket over a chair and pulls the suspenders off his shoulders. He struggles with the damn fat suit but quickly pulls that off too.

Candace knows Nick is right. She just blew up her whole plan two weeks before Christmas.

She's not sure how it happened.

All she knows is Nick's stripped down to a tight black t-shirt in her office. And he's angry.

And he said he doesn't like any of the women who've been sitting on his lap.

And he hasn't been with Mary Johnson.

Candace's mouth is dry. "I, um… I think you should go. She nods toward his red velvet pants and boots. "You can turn in the rest of your suit on Monday."

"I'll give it to Dudley," he tells her as he storms out.

PART NINE

The Storm

Candace starts collecting the Santa gear that's been flung around her office.

She plucks Santa's hat from the potted plant on her desk.

She hates that Nick always gets the better of her.

She pulls the fat suit out of the trash can where it fell.

Up to this point in her career she's always prided herself on acting professionally.

She picks Santa's jacket off the floor and without thinking brings it to her nose. It smells like the forest. It smells like Nick.

Three little scraps of paper fall to the floor:

Stick to the Manual

In sparkly red and green ink.

Suddenly, Candace worries she's read him wrong.

She hasn't been fair.

She doesn't want to leave it this way.

Rushing out of the corporate offices with Santa's hat in her hand, she's surprised to find the mall completely empty. The lights have been dimmed except for the ones twinkling around Christmas Village.

All she hears is her own breathing, the wind howling... and the resounding echo of Santa boots heading for the east exit.

Candace runs to catch up to him. "Nick?"

"Fuuuuuuck. Fuck, fuck, fuck, fuck, *fuck*."

"Just let me apologize. Please - "

"This is not happening." Nick leans his head against the door and tries to open it as Candace catches up to him.

She looks through the glass at a total whiteout.

Nick pushes against the door but it doesn't budge. Candace throws herself against it, but it's no use.

When they both give it their all, it opens just enough that a mix of snow and wind knocks them to the ground. Then it slams shut again.

Nick scowls at Candace.

"You know -" she starts to explain.

"This is all -" Nick continues.

"- your fault!" they both finish, glaring at each other.

Nick's phone rings. *Mother Lovin' Mother* echoes through the mall.

"Are you okay, Nicky?" His mother sounds frantic."You're not driving in this, are you? You need to get yourself inside as soon as possible. They're saying it's going to be the worst storm in twenty years."

He closes his eyes. He sighs. "Fuck."

"Nicholas Barnabas Frost!"

"Sorry, Mom, I'm just-" As Nick opens his eyes, he realizes Candace isn't glaring anymore. She's trying not to laugh.

"Barnabus?" she mouths.

The crooked way her mouth turns up when she's attempting to stay in control is too much for him. He smiles back and shrugs.

"Nicholas, are you alright? Did you run off the road?"

"I'm okay, Mom. I'm at the mall."

"Oh, good, is Candace there?" she asks.

He tries his best not to make eye contact with the woman his mother adores.

Who *he* adores.

And fails.

He can't look away.

"She's here."

"Thank God! At least if you're with Candace I know she'll take good care of you."

Candace goes from smirking to openly grinning. She brushes her nails on her lapel and folds her arms across her chest.

Nick sighs, defeated. "I'll call you tomorrow."

He slips the phone into his back pocket and pushes himself up off the floor.

"Don't let it go to your head," he tells Candace, offering her a hand. "She still thinks poinsettias are deadly,"

"But they are," she argues as she lets Nick help her up. They head back toward the atrium.

Nick laughs. "Holly berries are more toxic than poinsettias."

"Whatever. I dare you to eat one," she says, twisting his Santa hat in her hands.

"No thanks."

"Cause they're poisonous."

"Because I don't make a habit of eating Christmas plants."

"Right. Because it would kill you."

Nick stops short. "Candace?"

It's the exact spot where Candace had her first kiss. Lights twinkle overhead. Snow covering the glass ceiling blocks out the stars.

"Yeah?" she asks breathlessly, twirling in a slow circle.

"Do you *always* have to be right?"

"Do you always have to prove me wrong?"

"I guess we both want to prove ourselves to people."

Candace stops spinning but the lights all around them are still a blur. The only thing she sees clearly is Nick standing in front of her. "Did we just find something we have in common?"

"Scary, but yeah, I think we did."

Nick is thoughtful as they head back toward Christmas Village. The quiet that falls between them gives him time to regret how his temper got the best of him, earlier.

"I'm sorry I said I hated the job back there. Truth is, it has its moments."

"Are you kidding? *I* hated your job. I'm sorry I put you through it. I just really wanted this to work out."

Nick really wanted it to work out, too. "So, we both have the compulsive trait of proving other people wrong..."

"Or right."

"Right," he agrees. "And we both *hate* the Santa suit."

"Speak for yourself. It's... not so bad."

Candace rearranges the ornaments on an evergreen in an attempt to hide her blushing cheeks.

"You're kidding, right?" He pulls at his suspenders. "This does it for ya?"

She's not sure why Nick's surprised. It did it for about two hundred women in the past two weeks.

"No comment." Candace smirks as she hands him his hat. "I guess we don't have anything else in common. I mean, Christian told me you hate it here."

Nick winces. He remembers saying it when he left. Tonight he's not sure he feels the same. "Hate's a strong word."

"He said you couldn't wait to get to California. Hated the cold. The winters. Even cranberries, for goodness sake."

"All true, I guess. At one point anyway."

"Are you trying to tell me you like those things?"

"Let's just say my hatred for cranberries has diminished slightly since coming back."

Candace pretends to gasp. "Is that a roundabout way of saying you actually *like* cranberries?"

"They're... not so bad." Nick grins as he flicks one of the low hanging, silver snowflakes that Candace has peppered throughout the mall. He catches his red-velvet covered reflection in one of the storefront windows. There's no way he's spending the rest of the evening looking like Santa's younger brother.

"Listen." He clears his throat. "I know how much you love the suit but... I really need to change if we're gonna be stuck here."

"I do *not* love - " she starts to say, before she notices Nick raising an eyebrow in challenge. Candace can't lie. "Sure thing. And I promise not to follow you in, this time."

Nick tries not to show his disappointment as he takes off for the locker rooms.

Instead of watching him go, Candace wanders through Christmas Village. Everything is back in its place. Everything except a little pile of liquor bottles at the foot of Santa's throne. As she picks them up to tidy things, Candace has an idea.

She heads to the hot chocolate station where she makes two spiked drinks, one with Bailey's, the other with whiskey. With another thought she adds a second shot to both mugs. Then she plucks two bags of pretzels from the shelf by the register and leaves enough cash so Jim will find a generous tip in the morning.

Back at the Christmas Village, Candace spots Nick in a snug wool sweater, jeans, snow boots, and his Santa hat. She thinks he looks hot... err... very warm. Appropriately dressed.

"You've really upped your winter game." She holds out the two mugs. "Bailey's or whiskey?"

"You should see the parka I have stashed. And definitely whiskey," he says as he takes the mug, then takes a sip.

He hums.

Candace feels it in her bones.

She looks for something to distract her from the man at her side. "So, what now? Looks like we're gonna be here for a while."

Two hours later, Nick and Candace relax on a fake snowdrift at the edge of Christmas Village. Nick leans against a lamppost. He's replaced his Santa hat with a borrowed pillow that's propped behind his head. Candace sits next to him, cross-legged, her head on his shoulder.

They've had two more spiked hot chocolates and shared a box of cranberry-filled truffles from Cranberry Cove.

Wind howls outside. Closing credits roll at the end of *Miracle on 34th Street*, projected on the wall across from them.

Candace tries to inconspicuously wipe tears from her eyes.

She's not fooling Nick, though. "It was a happy ending, you know that right?"

Candace sniffles as she looks him over. "I don't know what I was thinking."

"About?"

"You're Nick Frost, not Kris Kringle. Not even close."

Nick sits up straight and puts a hand to his chest. "Ouch."

"No, I just mean Santa's not supposed to be sexy."

He waves a hand at the projector. "He's also not supposed to be...wait. What?"

"I was so caught up in blowing my projections out of the water I lost track of what this is all about. I should never have pimped Santa out for Christmas, Nick. I'm so sorry."

Candace pulls some tissue paper from a decorative gift bag and blows her nose.

"Hey... hey, it's okay." Nick slips an arm around Candace's shoulders. He pulls her close. She buries her face into his chest as he speaks softly. "The important thing to remember here is, you think I'm sexy."

"Wait." Candace puts some space between them and stares at Nick, confused. *"What?"*

Nick holds his hands up. "You said it."

"That's not what I... I mean... I don't... Maybe *Mary Johnson* -"

"I mean, if you'd told me before I was fired it could be a problem. But now..."

Nick is teasing but Candace looks anything but amused. In fact, if he isn't mistaken, she looks... interested.

"But now *what*?" she wonders.

Nick hesitates. "Now..."

He feels the same pull that's been there since the day they met. A pull he hasn't let himself act on. Until now.

He leans in.

"Now?" she asks, searching his eyes.

"Now," he whispers, brushing his lips against hers.

She tastes like Baileys and hot chocolate. She smells like cranberries. She feels soft and warm pressed against him as she climbs onto his lap.

Finally.

"Now," she whispers in his ear.

Candace's lips leave goosebumps in their wake.

Nick closes his eyes, he wraps his arms around her, fists her sweater and breathes her in.

When he loosens his hold and looks into Candace's eyes, he feels like the universe has finally given him something good again.

Something great.

He smiles wistfully.

Candace raises an eyebrow.

Then it hits him. "Oh you mean *now*."

Candace can't hold back any longer. Her lips crash into Nick's and two weeks worth of pent-up sexual tension is unleashed on the floor of the Oak Grove Mall. She tears at his sweater, pulling it up and over his head, only to find a flannel underneath.

She giggles, her lips still against his.

"I blame Wisconsin's sub zero winters," Nick confesses.

Candace struggles with buttons like she's unwrapping the most annoying and amazing Christmas gift ever. Giggles evolve to full on laughter when she finds a thermal t-shirt underneath the flannel. "You're too much. Like all these layers are literally too much."

"Be grateful I didn't leave the Santa suit on."

Nick can't imagine this going well with that thing to contend with.

Candace shrugs. Her cheeks flame.

"Maybe next time?" Nick suggests.

"I wouldn't mind," Candace admits as he fiddles with the clasps running down the back of her sweater.

"I'm not sure which is worse, my layers or your buttons."

In answer, Candace pulls the sweater over her head and tosses it aside where it dangles from the nearest faux-snow covered evergreen.

Nick stares at it for a split second. "Yeah that would have made a lot more sense."

When he turns his attention back to the woman straddling his lap, he's in awe. Candace is sweaterless and beautiful, in a red lace bra. Her skirt has slid almost to her hips.

That's gonna need to go, too.

Candace bites her bottom lip as she reaches behind her back to unclasp her bra. She shrugs the straps from her shoulders, but holds the rest of it in place over her chest.

The intimacy of that small movement is all the invitation Nick needs.

He pulls the bra out of her hand and flings it, only vaguely aware that it's landed in the Christmas tree nearby. Then he grabs ahold of her and tries to push the two of them off of the floor, only to topple them over into a huge pile of fake snow.

Candace can't help but laugh.

Nick buries his face into her neck. "So much for trying to be cool about this."

"This isn't California, Nick. I don't need cool. I just need you."

She grabs a handful of snow and sprinkles it over their heads. Lights twinkle overhead in place of stars, as the projector moves on to the opening scene of *It's a Wonderful Life*.

"California's got nothing on you," he swoons.

Their next kiss is softer, sweeter.

It's the kiss Candace has been fantasizing about since the moment they met.

As it builds, Nick's nerves begin to fade. Candace pulls him closer. She can't get enough, not when she hitches her leg over his thigh, not when he slides a hand between her legs, not when she feels him hard against her through four layers of clothing.

As Nick attempts to unzip Candace's skirt, she tries to help by rolling on top of him. When she goes for his jeans, he rolls on top to help *her*, and the two of them roll down Candy Cane Lane, past the hot cocoa station, until they smack into the evergreen that holds the entire Christmas Village together. Mostly naked.

Snow and ornaments rain down around them.

"This isn't gonna work," he mutters.

"Oh my goodness. Yeah. Sorry," Candace says, trying to scoot away from him. She can't believe she got so carried away. They've scattered their clothing everywhere.

Nick holds her tight. He smiles. "I mean on the floor, Candace. This isn't gonna work… on the *floor*." He kisses her again to drive the thought home. Then he stands, naked as a jaybird, and helps Candace up.

"Not on the floor, huh?" Candace nods to Santa's throne.

Nick thinks that's a great idea.

He takes Candace's hand in his and begins to back his way toward it. Then promptly slips on the Santa hat he tossed aside earlier, and falls onto the chair like a great, golden, naked Santa.

Candace plucks the hat off the ground as Nick pulls her onto his lap. "Keep it on for me?"

Nick smirks. "Is *that* your Christmas wish?"

"Might be part of it."

Candace places the hat on Nick's head with care.

Nick adjusts his glasses. "Granting wishes is kinda my thing."

"Is that so?" Candace asks as she slides her arms around his neck. "Any idea what else I want?"

"I certainly hope so." Nick reaches for Dudley's secret stocking, hanging from the fireplace, no more than a foot from Santa's throne.

Candace wasn't expecting an actual gift. At least, not more than the man underneath her.

When Nick pulls a condom from the stocking, her mouth falls open.

"You have no idea how much action that elf gets around here," he admits.

Candace does her best to put that piece of information out of her mind considering she's straddling Santa naked. Workplace rules have clearly gone out the window for the night.

"I think you're getting the hang of this." She plucks the package from his hands and tears it open.

"Well, I did have a good trainer." Nick holds his breath as Candace slowly rolls the condom onto him.

"There's one last part to my wish," she coos as she lifts her hips, then lowers herself just enough to tease.

"Fuck."

"Right again, Santa," she says, sinking down slowly, deliberately.

When she begins to move against him, Nick clenches her hips, steadies the pace, careful not to rush this, desperate to feel every inch of himself inside her.

He gazes into Candace's eyes.

He tries to breathe.

"You're fucking gorgeous, you know that?"

Candace can't speak. Instead she presses her lips to his as her heart hammers, his hands clutch, and they find their rhythm.

Nick traces the curves of Candace's body. Over her hips, along her waist, until he cups a breast. Candace sighs against his mouth.

Cupping turns to pinching. Pinching to pulling.

Sighs turn to humming. Humming to moaning.

She moves against him with purpose, so soft, so warm, so *right*. Her hair tickles his face. Her nails dig into his shoulders and it feels... so... good.

And she sounds... so close.

And smells like cranberries.

It's all too much.

Nick can't get enough.

"Christ."

Candace arches her back, tips her hips, then tightens her thighs around him.

Nick won't last much longer.

He slips a hand between the two of them and it's all Candace needs to push her over the edge.

Nick curses as he comes, but it's drowned out by Candace's voice. Her cries of Christmas cheer echo all the way to the food court.

"Ho, ho, *woah*," Nick says with a chuckle.

Candace giggles. "Merry Christmas, Santa."

"Christmas wish fulfilled?"

Candace shrugs, playing coy. "Almost…"

Nick's lips pout. His brow knits. His eyes dip.

He's about to apologize for not getting it right when Candace finishes her thought. "I wish we had more condoms."

That he can handle.

Nick reaches into Dudley's secret stocking again and pulls out an entire Trojan Pleasure Pack. "Is this enough?"

"I was so wrong about you, Nick Frost," she says, straightening his red velvet hat. "You turned out to be the best Santa ever."

About the authors

Marie and Jo have been making each other laugh for over a decade and have been writing together for three years. While Jo has a few published works out in the world, they will soon be publishing their first works as a writing team.

During the day, Marie runs a small medical practice and teaches future doctors. Jo manages projects for a fast-paced tech company. Together they leave workday stress behind to create imaginative, heartfelt stories with a pinch of angst, a little grit, a dash of drama, and just enough humor to make it all better.

Follow Marie & Jo on Facebook:
https://www.facebook.com/marieandjowrite

Dearest Reader,

The best way to support Indie Authors is to leave a review. If you enjoyed this story, please consider visiting Marie & Jo's Amazon page and letting them know.

Thank you!

Made in United States
Orlando, FL
30 December 2024